Gabby Runs Away

by Michèle Dufresne

Pioneer Valley Educational Press, Inc.

Matt and his friends were playing basketball.

Gabby wanted to go
for a walk.
She looked at the boys.
"Woof, woof," barked Gabby.

"Go away Gabby," said Matt.
"We are busy playing basketball.
We are too busy
to play with you now."

Gabby was sad.
"Woof, woof," said Gabby.

Gabby looked up
the driveway.
Then she looked
at the boys.
They were not looking at her.

Gabby started up
the driveway.
Then she looked
at the boys again.
They were not looking.
They were too busy
playing basketball.

Mom came out of the house.
"Boys, where is Gabby?
I am going to take her
for a walk."

The boys looked around.

"Gabby, Gabby!
Come here," called Matt.

Gabby did not come.

"Oh no," said Matt.
"Maybe she went up
the driveway!"

"Oh no!" cried Mom.
"Maybe she is in the road."

Matt and Mom
ran up the driveway.

"Gabby, Gabby! Come!" they called.

"Gabby, where are you?"
called Mom.

Gabby was in the road!
"Oh no!" cried Mom.
"A car is coming!
Will they see little Gabby?
Bad dog! Come here, Gabby."

Gabby sat in the road and looked
at the car. She did not come.

"Do you want to go
for a walk, Gabby?"
asked Matt.

"Woof, woof," barked Gabby,
and she ran to Matt.
"Oh, good dog," said Matt.